The Lone Little Leaf

Archway Publishing books may be ordered through booksellers or by contacting:

Archway Publishing
1663 Liberty Drive
Bloomington, IN 47403
www.archwaypublishing.com
844-669-3957

Because of the dynamic nature of the Internet, any web addresses or links contained in this book may have changed since publication and may no longer be valid. The views expressed in this work are solely those of the author and do not necessarily reflect the views of the publisher, and the publisher hereby disclaims any responsibility for them.

ISBN: 978-1-6657-4332-7 (sc)
978-1-6657-4333-4 (e)

Library of Congress Control Number: 2023908095

Print information available on the last page.

Archway Publishing rev. date: 01/03/2024

ARCHWAY
PUBLISHING

The Lone Little Leaf

Written By:

Susan Kay Marak Jones

This book is dedicated to my family who has always supported me through school and my friends at work that encouraged me to write this down, and Prof. Wiseman, who gave me a reason for finally doing it.

As I look up above me, and I see,
A lone little leaf, left up in a tree.

He waves and shakes, along in the breeze,
All by himself, with no other leaves.

He must be tough, to hold on so long,
His siblings let go, and away they've gone.

He's no longer green, but a brilliant yellow,
A rather cheery handsome, and charming little fellow.

But the weather is shifting, soon it will be cold,
Will the wind whisk him away, or will he stay for the snow.

But he will endure, because he is strong,
Until he knows it's time, to bravely move on.

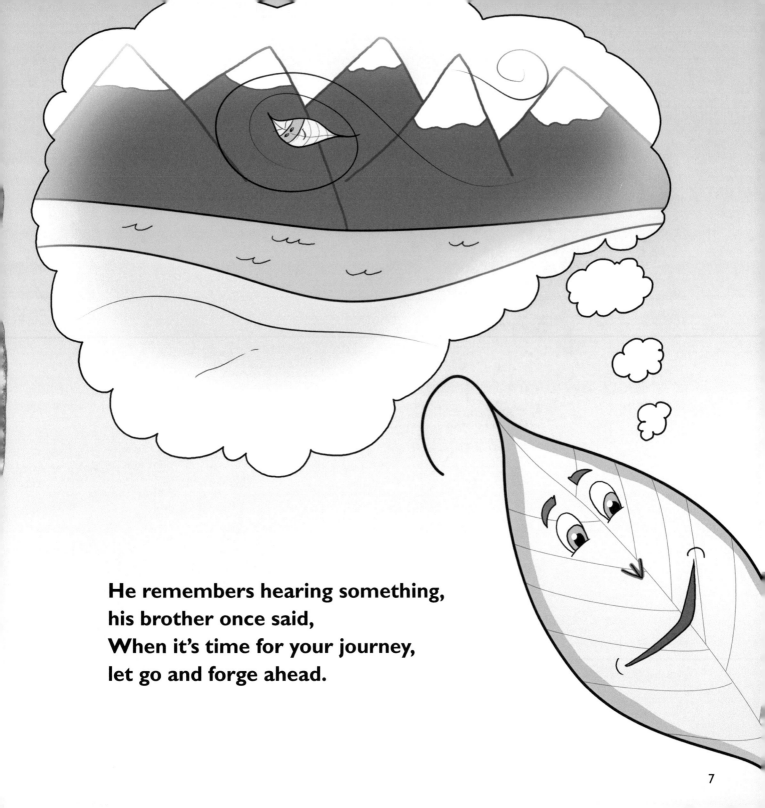

He remembers hearing something,
his brother once said,
When it's time for your journey,
let go and forge ahead.

We all must leave, this place we call home,
But it will be okay, because we're never alone.

As buds we were nurtured, from roots, trunk and branches,
Knowing someday we'd let go, and take our chances.

9

There's new adventures, animals and people to meet,
Maybe a small town, or a busy city street.

Believe in yourself, you'll know when it's time,
To search for your destiny, you'll be just fine.

**Now I sit outside, this fine fall day,
Under this big tree, I just want to say.**

As I look up to the branches, at my little friend,
A gust of wind whips up, and down he descends.

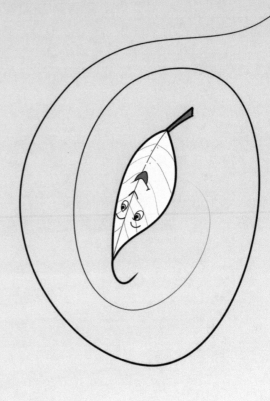

**But the airstream catches him, in her gentle arms,
He dances away, by Mother Nature's charms.**

I wonder what sights, my friend the leaf will see,
I can only guess, but dream some day it will be me.

Printed in the United States
by Baker & Taylor Publisher Services